W9-CAX-303

Kitty Cat, Kitty Cat,
Are You Waking Up?

BY **Bill Martin Jr** and **Michael Sampson**

ILLUSTRATED BY **Laura J. Bryant**

SCHOLASTIC INC.
New York Toronto London Auckland
Sydney Mexico City New Delhi Hong Kong

No part of this publication may be reproduced, stored in a retrieval system, or transmitted in any form or by any means, electronic, mechanical, photocopying, recording, or otherwise, without written permission of the publisher. For information regarding permission, write to Marshall Cavendish, 99 White Plains Road, Tarrytown, NY 10591.

ISBN-13: 978-0-545-20787-4
ISBN-10: 0-545-20787-8

Text copyright © 2008 by Michael Sampson and Bill Martin Jr.
Illustrations copyright © 2008 by Laura J. Bryant.
All rights reserved. Published by Scholastic Inc., 557 Broadway, New York, NY 10012, by arrangement with Marshall Cavendish. SCHOLASTIC and associated logos are trademarks and/or registered trademarks of Scholastic Inc.

12 11 10   12 13 14/0

Printed in the U.S.A.   40

First Scholastic printing, September 2009

The text of this book is set in Classical Garamond.
The illustrations are rendered in watercolor paints and colored pencils on Strathmore paper.
Book design by Anahid Hamparian
Editor: Margery Cuyler

To *my cat-loving niece, Leslie*
—M.S.

To *the many kitty cats that have napped on my lap*
—L.J.B.

Kitty Cat, Kitty Cat,
are you waking up?

"Not yet, Mother,
I'm a sleepy buttercup."

"Kitty Cat, Kitty Cat,
are you out of bed?"

"Not yet, Mother,
I'm standing on my head."

"Kitty Cat, Kitty Cat,
have you cleaned your fur?"

"Not yet, Mother,
I'm practicing my purr."

"Kitty Cat, Kitty Cat,
what are you going to wear?"

"Just a second, Mother,
I'm looking everywhere."

"Kitty Cat, Kitty Cat,
where'd you put your socks?"

"Just a second, Mother,
they're over by my blocks."

"Kitty Cat, Kitty Cat,

have you found your shoes?"

"Just a second, Mother,

they're easy things to lose."

"Kitty Cat, Kitty Cat,
do you want some fish?"

"Just a second, Mother,
I'm playing with my dish."

"Kitty Cat, Kitty Cat,
hurry up and eat."

"Just a second, Mother,
a mouse is on my seat!"

"Kitty Cat, Kitty Cat,
you'll be very late!"

"Just a second, Mother,
school will have to wait."

"Kitty Cat, Kitty Cat,
now we have to go!"

"Okay, Mother,
I'm sorry I'm so slow."